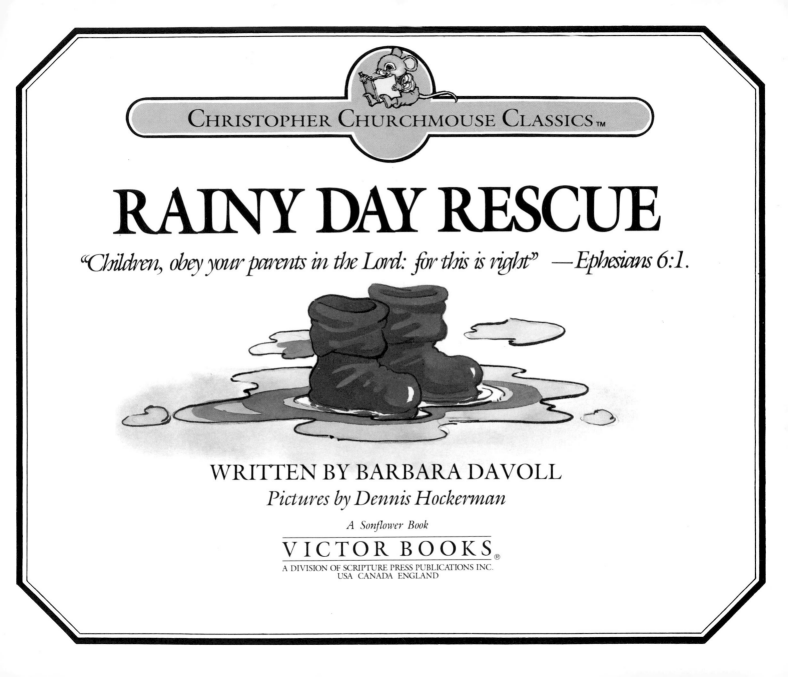

# CHRISTOPHER CHURCHMOUSE CLASSICS™

# RAINY DAY RESCUE

*"Children, obey your parents in the Lord: for this is right"* —*Ephesians 6:1.*

## WRITTEN BY BARBARA DAVOLL
*Pictures by Dennis Hockerman*

*A Sonflower Book*

# VICTOR BOOKS®
A DIVISION OF SCRIPTURE PRESS PUBLICATIONS INC.
USA CANADA ENGLAND

CHRISTOPHER CHURCHMOUSE CLASSICS

*Saved by the Bell*
*The White Trail*
*A Sunday Surprise*
*The Potluck Supper*
*A Load of Trouble*
*Rainy Day Rescue*

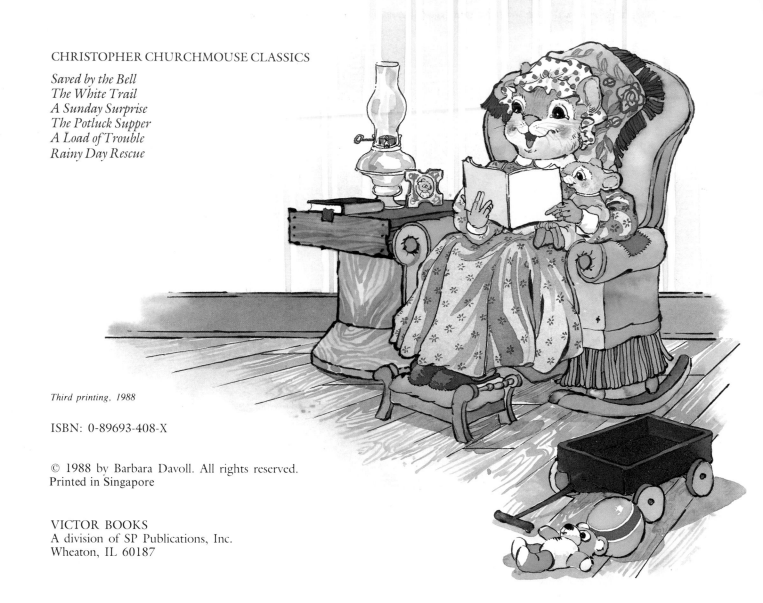

*Third printing, 1988*

ISBN: 0-89693-408-X

VICTOR BOOKS
A division of SP Publications, Inc.
Wheaton, IL 60187

# A Word to Parents and Teachers

The Christopher Churchmouse Classics will please both the eyes and ears of children, and help them grow in the knowledge of God.

This book, *Rainy Day Rescue,* one of the character-building stories in the series, is about obedience. Christopher and his friend, Ted, discover that obedience is always best.

> *"Children, obey your parents in the Lord:*
> *for this is right"* —Ephesians 6:1.

The Discussion Starters will help children make practical application of the biblical truth. Happy reading!

Christopher's Friend,

*Barbara Davoll*

hristopher Churchmouse watched the rain come down. *Would it ever stop?* he thought. *What a day!* There was nothing to do.

"Mama, what can I do?" he asked.

"Why don't you go outside and play?" asked Mama Churchmouse. "It isn't raining very hard. Get one of your cousins to play with you."

"All right," said Christopher, grabbing his raincoat and hat.

"But Christopher, listen to me. You may play outside in the puddles, but don't go in the storm sewers. They are very dangerous."

"Yes, Mama. I'll remember," said Christopher, and out the door he went.

4

Soon Ted and Chris were sloshing around in the yard in their little boots, making the water splash.

"Hey, we should have done this sooner. This is a lot of fun," said Ted.

"Yeah," said Christopher, "I'm glad Mama thought of it."

After awhile, Ted said to Christopher, "Hey, look over here." He was on the curb, at the side of the street, peeking down into the storm sewer.

5

"No, Ted, we'd better not go over there. My mom said that's a dangerous place for a mouse. She said not to go off the curb."

"Aw, come on," said Ted, taking a jump and landing smack in the middle of the long puddle that ran along the curb. "Hey, Christopher, this is really neat."

6

Christopher took one look and thought, "Well, Mama said not to go in the sewer. She didn't say we couldn't play by it." And so, taking a big jump, he landed beside Ted.

"This is really fun!" cried Christopher.

Suddenly Christopher shouted, "This water's getting deeper!"

"Naw, it's just your imagination."

"Look, it's raining harder now," said Christopher. "Maybe we should go back in the house."

"No," said Ted. "We're just starting to have fun. Come on."

If the little mice could have seen the muddy, rushing water coming toward them, they would have jumped out and headed for home. But they couldn't see it.

7

All of a sudden they heard a great roar.

"What's that noise? It sounds like a train," said Christopher.

At that instant a muddy brown wall of water struck them full force.

"Hey, what is it? Where did that water come from?" cried Ted.

"I don't know. Help! Help me!" cried Christopher. "I'm falling."

"I can't!" shouted Ted. "The water is carrying me! What's happening?"

The water rushed along getting deeper and deeper. Christopher had all he could do to hold his head up out of the water.

8

"We're going to drown, Ted!" screamed Christopher. "See if you can grab something."

"There's nothing to grab. We're going down the storm sewer!" yelled Ted.

"Oh, no!" squealed Christopher as he was swept over into the blackness. "Help! Help! Mama! Papa!" But Mama and Papa could not hear.

"Ted, where are you? I can't see you."

"I can't see you either. I'm over here," said Ted, trying to keep his head above water. "Oh, Christopher, I'm so scared."

"Don't worry, Ted. Try not to be frightened," said Christopher.

All of a sudden the boys landed upon something very hard. They had dropped onto a little shelf of broken sewer tile. At that moment they saw a tiny glimmering light moving toward them.

"Christopher, what's that light?"

"I—I don't know. Just be quiet."

The boys' eyes were round with fear as they saw coming toward them a pack of the biggest rats they had ever seen. They were terribly mean looking and one was carrying a lantern.

"Well, what do we have here?" said the leader. "Look at these little mice babies."

"They ought to be good for some fun," said one of the rats.

"Who are they?" whispered Ted.

"Water rats, I think," said Christopher. "They live here in the sewer."

Coming closer, the leader of the pack stepped up and said, "Where did you sweet little things come from?"

"We were washed down the sewer."

"Ha, ha, ha," laughed the big rat. "Did you hear that, rats? They were washed down the sewer. Didn't your mommies tell you not to play near the storm sewer?"

"Yes, yes sir, but we . . ."

"Ah, ha, ha! You didn't obey your mommies, did you?"

"N—no—no, we didn't."

"Oh, that's the first step to becoming mean, ugly sewer rats like we are, right?"

"Right!" chorused the rats.

"Well, now that they're here with us they can be our little servants, can't they?"

"What we mean is that you can run our errands and do everything for us, and pretty soon you'll grow up to be just as mean as we are. We'll be back and then we'll have some fun things for you to do." And the rats left.

"Oh, no," said Christopher.

"Oh, Christopher, I'm so scared," said Ted. "Whatever will we do? We can't get out of here."

"It will be all right," said Christopher, with a bravery that he did not feel. His eyes became accustomed to the darkness. Chris saw that the little shelf of broken tile left them no room to spare. There was no way for them to get out. They were trapped.

"Oh, why didn't I obey my mama," moaned Christopher.

"It's all my fault," said Ted. "You didn't want to go down into the street to play."

"I know, but I shouldn't have listened to you. Mama told me it was dangerous, and I should have obeyed."

"Well, no use thinking about that now," said Ted.

They sat down and soon Ted fell asleep on Christopher's shoulder. Christopher sat staring into the dark, wondering if this would be the end of his life. All of a sudden Christopher heard a scratching sound.

*Oh, what is that,* he wondered in fear.

"Ted! Ted, wake up. There's a noise. Listen."

"Maybe it's the r—rats coming back," stammered Ted.

"I don't think so. This noise is behind us. It's different than the noise the rats made," said Christopher.

The scratching got closer and closer. The mice boys huddled together.

"Is that you, Christopher?" said a scratchy, familiar voice.

"Murky," said Christopher. "Is that you, Murky? It's Murky Mole!" he squeaked. "Where are you, Murky? I can't see you."

"Here I am," said Murky, as he nosed his way through the soft dirt right to where Chris and Ted were sitting. "I dug down here to get you," said Murky.

"How did you know where we were?"

"I watched you boys going down into the street to play and I thought to myself that you shouldn't be down there," said Murky. "And I knew about this little shelf. I thought you might have landed here."

"Oh, Murky, you were right. Mama told me not to play in the street. But we did, and a wall of water washed us down here and some awful rats came."

"I know," said Murky, "and the rats will be back soon. If we don't get out of here now, you'll be held prisoners. We must go."

"But Murky, how did you do it?"

"I'm a mole," said Murky proudly. "I can tunnel under the ground."

Christopher looked at his cousin Murky, who was covered with dirt. He remembered that he used to make fun of Murky because he preferred to be underground. Christopher felt ashamed. He knew Murky was being very kind.

17

"I'll get you out," said Murky, "if I made the tunnel big enough. If I didn't, I'll just make it bigger."

"Oh, Murky, that is wonderful of you," said both mice.

"No problem for a mole," said Murky proudly. "Let's go. Chris, grab hold of my tail and then, Ted, you grab hold too. Follow me!"

"All set!" shouted Christopher.

"It's going to be tough climbing. I know you guys aren't moles. I'll go as slowly as I can."

Then began the long climb back up through the earth. The soil got into the eyes and fur of the little mice. They seemed to climb for hours.

Suddenly Ted said, "Christopher, look! There's a light up ahead!"

"We're almost out," said Murky.

"Oh, Murky! Thank you. You're wonderful!" said Christopher.

"Think nothing of it," said the mole, pushing ahead.

As they crawled through the hole, squinting at the bright light, Christopher was astonished to see his whole family standing there in the rain.

"Mama, Papa—how did you know where we were?" asked Christopher.

"Murky told us," said Mama. "He told us so that we wouldn't worry. We knew he was going after you."

"Oh, Mama," said Christopher, sobbing. "I'm so ashamed."

Aunt Snootie and Uncle Rootie were hugging Ted and trying to brush the mud and dirt off his face.

Mama took her handkerchief and wiped Christopher's face. "Oh, Chris, why did you disobey me? Do you know that it is a miracle you didn't drown? If Murky hadn't seen you, none of us would have known where to look for you."

"I know, Mama," sobbed Christopher. "I am so sorry that I disobeyed.

Are you going to paddle me?"

"No," said Mama. "Not now. We'll talk later. I think you probably have had enough for one day."

"I'm so glad you're safe," said Papa, giving Christopher's paw a squeeze.

"Me too," said Christopher.

"And I hope you've learned your lesson about obedience."

"Oh, I have, Papa. I've learned that when Mama says not to do something it's not because she wants to spoil my fun. It's because she really has a good reason."

"That's right, Chris," said Papa.

"You must learn to obey even when you don't understand."

Papa went to Murky and shook his paw. "We can't ever thank you enough, Murky!"

And with that Mama and Papa took their cold, wet little mouse home. Christopher Churchmouse had learned a lot about obedience. He had also learned what *not* to do on a rainy day.

## DISCUSSION STARTERS

1. Why were Christopher and Ted so unhappy?
2. What did Mama Churchmouse tell them *not* to do?
3. What did they do? What should they have done to obey her?
4. What happened to the two mice because they disobeyed?
5. What kept them from drowning when they were swept away by the water?
6. Whom did they meet in the storm sewer?
   Then who came to rescue them?
7. What does God say about obedience to parents?